If We Could Hold Up The Sky

If We Could Hold Up The Sky

Kathryn Rossati

Contents

We'll be Atlas and hold up the sky,
together, always, you and I.

You

Hidden Flowers

It's time to flower now.
You've been waiting, I know.
It's daunting, revealing who you really are,
unaware as to how people will perceive you.

They'll wonder which section of roots
is really you.

Which you is the one they'll like most.

For those who love illusions,
your natural blooms will be devastating.
      For those who crave to see behind the faux foliage,
your blooms
will be vibrant, soulful trumpets.

Here We Are, My Friend

So you want to know
what your closed eyes are missing?

Grasp my hand and I'll show you.

I'll guide you down to the stream
and let you dip fingers in cool water,
feel how rocks break and curl the flow,
how small fish shy from your wake.

I'll lead you up obscure hill paths:
hold your arms out wide
so wind can sweep you up, and drop
you easily among long grasses and fallen catkins
that kiss your skin.

I'll take you to forests where rain has just eased
and the scent of crisp leaves on wet earth
rises to meet us with every stride,
where birds, deep in song, flit overhead
and squirrels scamper up trees;
chitter when you stray too close.

After all that,
I'll draw your hands to my smiling face:
feel each muscle lift, each eye crease deepen,
each cheek warm
as you process, blink,
and lock your gaze with mine.

Observations Of A Face

Each muscle contorts to form an expression,
a one-sided twitch creates a half-smile
that exposes your teeth
enough to lightly rest the backs of your fingers against them;
pensive as always,
staring off into the distance.

Sometimes   your eyes are mild: a lake on a still afternoon.
They can change in a beat,
build an intensity as great as a maelstrom
threatening to swallow ships headed its way.

Soft brows cannot hide waves of emotion, threatening to crash;
only practice and willpower   make them bow down.

Those cheeks are always lifted in a grin,
but ache, wonderfully,
from a true   smile.

Skin Deep

I have seen your self-inflicted shackles:
faded bracelets where each bead
has been imbued with the power to restrict
a part of your personality
in an act of self-protection.

Worn for so long they've merged with your skin,
only those with a trained eye
can see them for what they are.

I couldn't. Not at first.
But over time you allowed me to notice.
Over time, you let slip.

And since that instant of understanding,
I've wanted nothing more than to ease them off you.
Not forcefully –
I don't want to wound you like those before:
without thought, without purpose, other than a few laughs
that I know still cut through you,
even though they are nothing,
and you are everything.

I want you to emerge fully,
bask in the light;
never feel the need
to bury yourself again.

Tranquillity

Balance, arms shoulder height.
The line is thin, yes. Knife-edge some days.
Overwhelm one side, fury on the other.

Don't worry, I'll catch you if you fall.
Lay you on the freshly-cut grass
to inhale its scent
and allow your barbeque of a shift
to blow away on the evening breeze.

You think you are *yin*,
always darkness with a touch of light.
    Who is to say
that dark isn't encouraging?
It could lead anywhere, to anything.
    A mystery.
Adventures
I can take part in   simply by holding your hand.

Lie with me on the ground.
Let us chuckle,
let us talk,
let us live.
Not just for now, in the moment:
forever –
    only a long way off
if you view it that way.
Shake up your viewfinder; dust the lens.

Fresh eyes on sunset.
Or is it dawn?

Craft Time (In Chuckling Bursts)

You say my laughter is infectious, but yours
is already catching.
When childish excitement submerges you,
overtaken by one of your passions,
my heart fills.

We express ourselves openly,
creative energy merging
like the fruit of an hour's Spirograph session.
All curves and criss-crosses, tight patterns
too often mistaken by others
as mere scribbles.

To be expected, I suppose. We're wired differently;
they don't speak our language.

Together, we have no embarrassment.
We simply are.
No way to avoid being us.
And us   is all we need.

Black Cobwebs

You're hurting. I can see it
as plain as if you were holding up a sign to the world
stating as much in broken brush strokes.

Except everyone else, regardless
of physical visual ability
(yes, including those boasting perfect sight),
is blind to it.

It takes rolling tears for them to understand
you can't keep trudging away daily,
that care-free smile – weighing several tonnes –
hiding real thoughts.
Pretending, pretending, pretending
everything is fine.

No rest. No sleep. No messages.
It's wounding you.
Slathering you in red.
Call it pain, anger, grief,
call it   love.

Because you love,
because you claim a degree of happiness –
that gives the illusion you have distanced yourself from the family circle
and don't want to be distracted from your new nest –
there's guilt.
Needless guilt.

Your wish was never to be left out of the loop; goings on kept from you
because they think you don't care
or don't have *time* to care.
You say, 'Of course I do!'
but they can't hear.

I have known that same guilt
and understand why it's there.

I hate it. Hate its vines snagging you,
wrapping your entire being in a cocoon of self-loathing.
The only thing I can do
is hold your hand, drink your words
and let you lean on me.

It's nowhere near enough.

Droplets

Little universes, rolling down your cheeks
as fragments
of this alien sensation,
this overwhelming cascade
named in four letters: love.

Fastened

You listen to my concerns.
Never too busy to meet me in the gaps between days,
even though you are pulled
      on strings,
           puppet
made to dance through the night
no matter how often you ask your boss to set you loose,
if only for a single evening.

In turn, I'll always listen to the inky parts of your mind,
not caring what hour it is.
Know this: I'm not going anywhere.
My___ feet___ are___ sewn___ onto___ the___ same___ track___ as___ yours
by my own hand.

Stone Marker

Your legs are folded in half lotus, a solid base
to reflect upon the long hours we spend apart,
searching to change the shape of our timelines.
Adjust the slots forming our rigid contracts.

As you muse, the walls separating us decay,
while simultaneously, new ones are built elsewhere.
Co-workers ask for every detail; with each question,
you lay another brick
to shut their gossiping tongues out.

They think your ears are equipped to take their remarks,
but their incessantness and authority's cold words
have you crumbling inside,
water building pressure,
pushing against the dam of your eyes.

The clock's ticking is constant,
and each day brings you closer to breaking.
When you do, the flood of raw feelings
will be the only thing that makes them accept
they've gone too far.

Unmasked Musketeer

The mask you always wore
hangs on the wall,
dust caught in the gaps of its fine sequins and folds of silk.
Its paint is chipped and framework cracked.
An antique, a reminder of the confident charade you maintained
at the cost
of your vital essence being drained fraction by fraction.

Now, emotion plays in the swell of your cheeks.
Tears long held back escape,
are caught and crystallised.
Examine the glimmers within them:
      uncertainty, of allowing yourself to be loved,
to have someone willing to witness all
and not give a damn about anyone else's opinion.

Those soul-scars
from dagger-tongue school ghosts,
the calcified emptiness inside
caused by a raging demon who once took control
to ease overload.

You are not the sum of your past troubles,
you are the culmination of *every* moment up to this point
and all the choices beyond.

The mask can sit and decay. It won't be needed again.

Me

Free Swimming Hour

Outside of my routine
and spent of all back-up dialog,
I stumble,
    trip,
        stagger,
            fall
further outside what society deems 'normal';
that precious collection of
small talk,
eye contact,
a soft touch to the arm or shoulder when consoling or greeting;
and into the 'weird', 'eccentric', 'childish' zones
spat like insults
while I flounder in the rapids
of my brain.

No-one extends a hand back up,
but you argue that's not what I need.

You offer flippers,
giving me chance to swim
and find my own flow.

Throw Me Your Voice

Your voice turns my head (no matter what task I'm engulfed in),
lifts my nose from any book.
Stills my shaking, anxious heart
when the murmuration of thoughts gets too much.

Whether here beside me
or a summoning born of memories,
you are the foundation of my support.

Bell Song

Do you think if I hit the well's dangling bell,
it'd open a portal to you?

That's what I'd wish for, in this place
that occupies one space   but appears, framed three weeks ago,
in my head and yours.

Even if it wasn't a portal, just an echo drifting by,
I'd be satisfied.
Edge closer, two pence coin ready, aim.
Strike true.

Dream Flash

The light flicks on, blinding;
its voice is a condescending yellow,
the colour of my headaches.
I'm pushed straight into a surge of movement and sound,
slicing my senses like shattered glass.
Feet scuffle, shuffle closer,
petty complaints battering my ears:
'This item's not the advertised price!'
'Why is the paint I need not on the shelf?'
'Your service is terrible, I want to speak to a manager!'

I dial an SOS
but no one answers.

Might as well be calling the moon.
At least I'd get a response instead of melting into nothingness
quicker than the Wicked Witch.

But then you're here, striding cool.
You take my hand, tell me *it's okay,*
and with a single wink, reduce the saturation ten-fold.

Such a simple gesture, yet
it helps me get through it all.

Frayed, Not Tattered

I've been searching my life-yarn for
traces
of individual threads,
so I can pluck each one
out, analyse it.
After years, they're starting to unravel, make sense.

The way I am *me*   is quite different to the way you are *you*,
though our bubbling-brook chatter declares us
parallel frequencies.

When first we approached this rainbow-stained infinity loop of a bridge,
I leapt onto it;
as I ran, you grinned
and followed.

I know you see me clearly
whether I untangle my threads or not.
      But I crave
to be laid bare and accepted by others.

So I place myself here   even though it's hard, even though
my frayed ends are on show.
It's time I stopped hiding.

Out Of The Fog

The bathroom mirror fog obscures my face,
coating it in a weariness I can normally conceal.
Droplets run down my reflection:
the watery line masquerading as my mouth
is as thin as my identity; as long as my fear.

You come in, edge open the window.
The glass clears as you anchor me; that watery line thickens into a solid grin.
Your warmth causes the fog to lift and crawl
into the open air.

Groundskeeper

i)
We live in a world where everything
is on display, a continual waving of flags.
All I want to do
is move away, find a quiet, cosy area
and carve into my personal space.

ii)
I find that empty patch of earth,
fit it with neat trellis; climbing roses and honeysuckle curled
around to release their scent
in a way that doesn't overload my nose.

iii)
Someone approaches: their foot catches on the border,
sending them sprawling
and flattening the entire thing.
Crumpled blooms, dangling stems.
A puddle of thorns.
That's all that's left.

iiii)
I'm standing in a mess of debris,
when I hear the call of a friend
(they have a key,
yet always ask permission to enter)
and I remember: I don't have to fix it alone.

They help sweep the mess away,
glue it all back together
until I feel myself again.

The Meaning Will Present Itself

Okay, okay.
I'm here now, present.
No, not a present to be toyed with by others,
pushed around until its shiny wrapping is tarnished
and full of holes.
I'm a silver-ribboned gift for myself, with a glittering tag reading
one word: neurodivergent.

I found the term on my own,
took it apart
and discovered each piece had a place on my skin.

I'm ready to show the pieces off,
arms weary from holding back.
Gosh, my traits are eager to be released.

I favour balance, truth, trust.
I dislike the smell of coffee in the morning,
toast is as bad.
Asking me to do something without proper instruction
is setting me up for disaster.

I don't like to be touched, cuddled, or kissed –
until I do.
And if I do,
know that it is because you   are one of the few I love,
one of the few I can suit up with
and ride beside into battle.

No longer will I stand beside those
who lean on me
without ever letting me lean back.

No apologies will be made
if anyone seeks to be offended
by my rising.

I am here. I am present.
I am my truest self.

Us

Naturally, We're Friends

The modulation of your voice is soothing,
and each gentle encouragement, each pause
to let me ponder before you begin again
when it's clear I'm struggling,
allows me to keep up with whatever idea you're expressing
at the time.

You give no judgement, no reason for me to gag
any part of who I am
because I'm 'not behaving appropriately'.

I'm comfortable in my movements when beside you
on our frequent strolls
along shaded sections of woodland.
I might not say much, but you pick up the white noise
I'm subconsciously drifting in, and float there with me
until we find a way to sharpen the image.

Platonic

Most of the time when we say,
'*I love you*',
it's directed at our spouse, our partner, our other half
but
what of all the other loves that fill us,
provide warmth, comfort, security?
What of the people
who make us feel accepted,
who enable us to rest at ease,
with whom we can't hide ourselves, even if we tried?
I think it's time we told them, too.
So here it is,
plain and simple:
I love you.

I'm Staying Right Here

When we're alone, your eyes communicate all I need to know;
they ask the most pertinent questions,
offer honest answers:

Are you okay?
Has someone upset you?
Work's getting to me.
I don't know how to utilize my creative energy anymore.

Then our celestial balance is thrown asunder
as everyone else comes into the room.
Casually waltzing into our little corner,
their conversations roar like oceans.
Up goes your invisible barrier, concealing
my best friend.

I remember
falling asleep to your heartbeat
pulsing against my ear.
You'll always let me in;
you gave me the entry code, after all.

Just don't leave it too long before asking me round.
That worry
and stress you keep bottled
needs to be set free.

We Are Alive

You are the music dancing around me. I step into it easily,
inhaling your earthy scent.
We fly, not plunge, into the beat's abyss,
colours fully splayed.

Where do we go now?

We could travel through wormholes,
and slip between the fabric of reality. It'd be safe,
we'd never lose sight of ourselves
because we construct our world upon each other.

How about building a castle?
Or should we try impersonating the Sphinx?
What if we settled inside a mountain
and sent tales of our travels
echoing to the surface
for scribblers to note down and make their own?

Maybe we'll continue to be kinetic.
Grow, even when we're already old.

'Maintain A Professional Manner' Spell

You're grinning at me.
I can tell it's real: it reaches your eyes.
We're working so closely that we could touch
if we wanted,
without moving a foot from our designated positions.

The checkouts we man
form either side of a horseshoe.
We stand to attention in the centre
scanning away our sanity.

And with their usual great insights,
our supervisors have decided to roll out a spell
which rids us of the ability
to form any meaningful words,
the expanse of our friendship locked painfully
into a prison of momentary interaction,
occurring in the ten seconds we're not being watched.

'Doing alright?'
'Surviving. Just.'

Snatched Moment In A Long Day

Toes touching, noses nuzzled,
magnetic hearts attracting.

The clock is ticking,
terrific eyes of the company's sly shadow
on our backs, recording every move.
We're a whisper away
from it coiling tendrils around our ankles
to drag us apart.

We form our circle, arm in arm,
our energy like salt
casting the cursed presence aside.

A beat more.
A beat more, and our lips touch.
A beat more, and we are.
We are, we are, we are.

Authority cannot break us.

Support

You've got my back; your firm hands grip my shoulders
as I tilt into you and filter the day's weight
from my limbs to yours. Not all of it,
but an even distribution.
We walk with our arms entangled;
our steps synchronised.
Vocalising thoughts
isn't necessary – they're in the twitch of our fingers,
the skip or slump of our feet,
the trust in our eyes.

Lazy Afternoon Rambles

As the week comes to a close,
    our schedules breathe
and I offer my hand
so we can touch palm to palm.

It would be a waste
if we didn't use this time to spark minds,

whether it takes a ramble in the mist
or an afternoon melting into the sofa
with sentences tumbling
from the waterfalls that we call lips.

Our Destination

Unexpected in many aspects, yet
hindsight, that smug devil,
yells there was never any possible way for us to avoid it:
the individual maps we used *appeared* different,
but after a chance question
– *would you like to meet up on a day off?* –
we overlaid them
and found they depicted the same area
from two unique perspectives.

Our legs have now been strengthened by hours hiking
each other's terrain
and tuning our radios in
to the babble of our over-wired heads.

Background Noise

Wherever we walk,
 the world quietens.
Be it through woods (filled with bird trills; scurrying mice),
 by the coast (crash of waves; confusion of holiday makers),
through a town (students resting after a packed college day),
or past families out for evening meals.

All of it dulls to a subtle hum
 in the wake of our path
and the intricately intimate maze of our minds.
Even though we know
we have to face the crescendo sometime,
 for the hours we stand together,
peace is all there is.

To You. The One In My Head. Always.

Who I've conversed with
in one way or another
since the day our platonic love,
our friendship,
our willingness to share all secrets,
hauntings, and scars, started.

Now, we are a couple.
Yes, it's true.

We had no barricades before.
We have no locks now.

I literally gave you a key,
because the idea of you coming to me
and finding the door
shut
was disturbing for us both.

You once asked
how I would feel if we didn't talk for a day.
I answered that I'd already tried it,
but you sent me a message
the very second I caved
and began composing my own.

Early Birds

Dawn. We kiss, say our good mornings. You, the boy who is my best friend, listen carefully to the account of my dreams and night terrors. You know where the parts come from, just as I do.

You understand me, inside and out, like the clockwork motion of cutting and shuffling your playing cards. But that took years of practice; we poured a jug of histories into a thimble.

We get ready for the day, planned and uncertain. We are a team, a cassette tape and pencil, always sorting out each other's flapping ribbons.

Us

A flick of the fingers,
an insight into the riddle,
a flutter of pages
and an eruption of giggles.

A silk-woven waistcoat,
a shuffle of cards,
a smile in your eyes,
and a melting of shards.

A morning of rambling,
a taste of trust-filled tart,
a hand offered in friendship
and a wide, open heart.

A letter revealing truths,
an evening of meditation,
a declaration made on both sides,
and a stop to our hesitation.

Unspoken

I like how our fingers latch
when they stray close.
There's no question or hesitation.
They simply link.

When words fail   because our throats bolt them in,
this small thing serves just as well.

It's an answer. An agreement.
An 'I'll stand beside you no matter what
you tell me, what sadness you release
or what traumas you carry'
contract.

And it's for life.

Shaken, Not Stirred

We're two sides of the same coin.
Individually an image, combined a complete person.
We could have gone forever being colleagues like any others,
without noting our potential for more.

But we were curious, too curious,
to heed our fear of rejection,
and over months of these niggling urges to reach out,
the right slot occurred.

A minute
in which we were alone in the cloak room
and you offered to teach me how to solve
a Rubik's cube
on our next day off.

After that,
the possibility of friendship slapped us repeatedly
until our cheeks were raw.

(Yes, we gave in and listened.)

Blanket Fort

It's a place built on whispers,
a cave crafted from dreams,
an escape from reality.

While we're there,
wrapped in darkness and each other's arms,
we're huddled safe, tranquil.

When we emerge, wings inflating,
we share the same markings,
our old wounds mere filigree.

Prism Song

The warmth from the window hits me in time with the tender touch of your fingers as they rest on my shoulder. In this moment, my eyes sweep over the words of a book you gave me, hungry for the story you knew I'd love. I glimpse the certainty of our future. It's always these small things,

  small comforts,

  that choke me up. I'm alive in your embrace. With you, dreams are achievable. My ambitions as a writer, crafter, green-fingered fiend, aren't met with snide remarks or disbelief. You acknowledge the spring of my creativity and bathe in it, giving me confidence to share crystals found in its waters.

Drop Your Guard

When you stand before someone
exactly as you are,
no armour, no shield,
and still find courage to investigate their face –
you are strong, raw, and real.
And when you let them do the same,
with no judgement,
understanding dawns for both of you.
        You might be terrified,
but opening chests that have long rusted shut
was never going to be easy.
All you can do is be the net
to catch each other's whole
as it spills forth and slips
through fingers.

Orienteering

Can we find our way without following
the carefully plotted routes of other's maps?
If our compass doesn't point North,
but to somewhere else entirely?

If we take each step hand in hand,
ignoring the suggestions fed to us
and being ourselves,
then our road may be as solid or fluid
as we like.

We won't always have a destination.
But we'll always have the journey.

After The Parade

There was a time when revealing any part of ourselves
to others
was something neither of us could do.
We experimented with smoke and mirrors, elaborate costumes
and overwritten performances;
handed out
cheap tickets to the circus act
we wanted to emit,
concealing, with flare and artful tongues,
the decrepit conditions behind the scenes.

Our painted grins have been scrubbed;
only our blemished, ruddy cheeks remain.
Au naturel: our smiles for each other
hold as much power as a thousand
strongmen lifting Ferris wheels.

Me; You

You accept me in all of my forms.

When I'm ecstatic and can't stop
flapping my hands and spinning around
(no matter how serious everyone is).

When I'm in a rage
burning to break everything –
but don't because logic kicks in; screams: 'that object is valuable!'

When I'm swamped
by sounds, sights, smells, my senses shutting down,
environment choking me   until I'm somewhere less bombarding.

When I'm so excited
that I weave you the story six times
over and the thrill is infectious,
though you have no personal investment.

When I can't grasp a 'simple' concept,
but run with advanced ones
that many of my peers have never heard of.

When I shed my façade
because I'm spent,
when I can no longer tell white lies
like *'I'm coping'*;
such fragile porcelain to begin with.

You accept
     me
and I'm shocked,
since, outside of family,
you're the first.

What A Difference A Chat Makes

In my sleep I keep drowning in storms:
throat fills with rain; vision dims.
I struggle into consciousness   to find
I still can't breathe.
The density of the clouds floating above my head
is thick enough to crush my spirit.

You visit. Not a shadow I've summoned,
not a memory.
Physically here.

Wielding your own version of Mjölnir – wit –
you disperse the clouds in an hour.

This isn't the first time.
Nor the second, third, fourth.
I doubt it will be the last.

But for now, you've given me the tools I need
to keep this ancient fog at bay.

Unruly Glands

Mountains root either side of my neck;
each head turn working the pain further in.
My mood is sepia,
and I worry it will stay that way.

But you are patient,
willing to overlook my frequent,
self-pitying remarks,
happy in the knowledge that I at least know
what I'm like
slumped against the day.

You bring buckets of music, games,
and discussions
of ridiculously funny family mishaps.
My colours return
when you wrap me in a blanket
embroidered with your heart's signature.

The Bard

Each word is the gateway into another,
pathways opening whenever his tongue runs wild.
Flashes of white: an unfaltering grin,
even when dark threatens to eat us up.

Every motion
has three words embedded in it,
a hallmark of our life –
we can't see how the years will play out,
but we trust in them.

Droplets of his musings cascade around me:
wetting the earth, the air,
and extracting stale thoughts
clogging up my psyche.

I cannot predict his tales, or rambling steps,
but I will listen and keep pace by his side.

Ten Of Hearts

Card-shuffler
Joke-maker
Smile-inducer
Chuckle-giver
Hand-holder
Maths-master
Code-weaver
Eye-twinkler
Barrier-breaker
Future-bringer.

Beyond

Clockwork Field

The breeze causes time to pause,
facial cogs jarred in a perpetual expression of bliss,
securing this moment in long grass
where we speak in tongues:
other languages no longer necessary.

Our minds criss-cross like latticework on a cherry tart,
promising sweetness but sometimes adding a sharp tang
just to shake things up.

Sky High

Breathing flares of words, turning to fire on tongues,
we're ready to light the trail ahead.
Determination powering our muscles, we   run
to the air balloon
that will soar
over the cloying, manipulating, ableist
throng –
who knock down our self-esteem every day,
add kindling to imposter syndrome
which already blazes
in our chests –
and transport us to a realm all our own.
There, we can write poetry,
construct and craft whatever we like
while the memories of our previous lives
burrow into the ground.

Chrono Surfers

1.
Morning shines across my eyelids,
and still your arms are clasped around me.
The whole night, you didn't let go.

The electricity in the lines of your face
sparks even brighter than the evening before.

2.
In my dreams, you're always present.
Mostly observing, there if I need you.
Yet a solid form none-the-less.

3.
I see your silhouette
on the horizon, glowing
with otherworldly light.
I snort, and you shuffle into shade, sharing my amusement.
We have no need for pedestals.
We are who we are,
more so when we're together.

4.
We don't compromise.
We ignite.

Not content with simply riding time's waves,
but making them.

Liquid Clay

You hand fits in mine so perfectly,
I wonder if they were cast from the same mould.

I can feel all of your soul
in the slightest touch.
I bathe in our thoughts of a future, thinking
one day,
one day.

The leaves are browning; copper, bronze, gold.
You are silver. A river of it,
a mirror
that I can swim in, to the house we'll have,
with a library,
a dojo,
and a room of puzzles only we can solve.

Trickster Time

It's a strange thing, time.
Hours   can feel like days
when you have something to look forward to,
someone to go home to,
     hold, cherish.

When you're with them, days
pass like minutes,
a hummingbird's pulse rolling the week along
so that once more you have to part.

Time, that careful trickster,
changes again,
making every second drag,
as if taking extra delight   in the stab wounds
separation causes you.

Butterfly Nets

I recall the fragrance of your hair
in a sprinkle of snatched privacy;
apple-scented value shampoo mixed with dusty knick-knacks,
a leftover from your bedroom.

The stars hovered high
though the moon hid itself under a shield of clouds.
Whispers of the breeze
rustled through our clothes as we spoke of adventures
where time wouldn't have to be caught
with butterfly nets,
and the key in my pocket would be ours,
not mine.

Foreshadow

As the antlers are shed
(no need for weaponry now,
we've driven off the gossipers for good),
the fog recedes from the footsteps we've left,
and the magnitude of our trek
blinks back into view.

Looking over the valley,
I see where the tributary we followed was birthed:
every droplet
gushing straight to the point we're at now
and continuing
fierce, full, and forever.

Make A Wish

Yes, it sucks
when our timetables clash –
I'm free Tuesdays and Fridays,
you, Wednesdays and Saturdays –
and true, we don't have any genie lamps
to summon each other during breaks,
but you can still
root through your memories and pluck out
my image:
my pout every time I fail to solve a riddle,
my delight when I finally manage to get one.

And a wish might not flag down a bus
that'll bring you directly to wherever I am,
but for now,
maybe it can give hope,
enough for us to draw into a tight embrace
while we wait for our paths to merge indefinitely.

Homely House

Strolling together;
a family of yours
is a family of mine.
Guffawing at insider jokes,
crafted from shared experience,
I think: we are from the same pit of clay,
just a year apart and
different blood in our veins.
We'll always speak our minds freely;
share every thought.

An Aromatic Infusion

We fly up hills and across sprouting fields,
forward ten years and back a few months,
all the while motionless, shoulder to shoulder.

The roads are curved,
always interlocking in the distance.
How many times have we faced this direction
and haven't noticed?

I envision us in a cottage
with a workshop made for inventing
and re-inventing.
Mathematical solutions and puzzles
poured into a teapot, with pages from a writer's notebook,
and left to brew.

The extracts merge wonderfully,
a full flavour
of the years we'll experience in a single cup.

Dear reader,

We hope you enjoyed reading *If We Could Hold Up The Sky*. Please take a moment to leave a review, even if it's a short one. Your opinion is important to us.

Discover more books by Kathryn Rossati at
https://www.nextchapter.pub/authors/kathryn-wells-fantasy-author

Want to know when one of our books is free or discounted? Join the newsletter at http://eepurl.com/bqqB3H

Best regards,
Kathryn Rossati and the Next Chapter Team

About the Author

Kathryn Rossati is an autistic and ADHD author of young adult and children's fiction, and a poet. She is a lover of books, dungarees, country walks, and is a Mother of Parrots.

Her other works can be found listed on her website:

www.kathrynrossati.co.uk

Lightning Source UK Ltd.
Milton Keynes UK
UKHW011841210521
384163UK00001B/83